Frogs'
Holiday

VIKING KESTREL
Penguin Books Ltd, Harmondsworth, Middlesex, England
Viking Penguin Inc., 40 West Street, New York, New York 10010, U.S.A.
Penguin Books Australia Ltd, Ringwood, Victoria, Australia
Penguin Books Canada Limited, 2801 John Street, Markham, Ontario, Canada L3R 1B4
Penguin Books (N.Z.) Ltd, 182–190 Wairau Road, Auckland 10, New Zealand

First published 1986
Text copyright © Margaret Gordon, 1986
Illustrations copyright © Margaret Gordon, 1986

British Library Cataloguing in Publication Data available
ISBN 0-670-80854-7

Printed in Great Britain by
William Clowes and Sons Ltd, Beccles.

Frogs' Holiday

Margaret Gordon

Viking Kestrel

There is a quiet, peaceful pond near here.

But for the frogs who live in the pond it is neither quiet nor peaceful.

There are too many big fish and too many small boys.

"We need to get away from this pond. We want a holiday," said the frogs one morning

So, taking some fly-and-spider sandwiches and flasks of pond-water, they hopped

up the hill and along the street in search of
the perfect place for a frogs' holiday.

They looked in the pet shop but that had
too many big fish.

They looked in the swimming-pool but that
had too many small boys.

Then they came to a place that was warm and damp. There were no big fish and no small boys.

It was Mrs Crumple's launderette. The frogs had found the perfect place for their perfect holiday.

They waited until
the last customer went home

and Mrs Crumple locked up
the shop and went upstairs. Then . . .

they had lots and lots of fun.

Mrs Crumple came back downstairs with a large bag of her own washing.

"What's going on?" cried Mrs Crumple.

"Out by morning!" ordered Mrs Crumple. "But we want a holiday," wailed all the frogs. "I NEED a holiday," said Mrs Crumple.

"Then off you go," said the frogs, "and we'll mind the shop and the baby as well."

So the next day the
frogs washed towels
for the hairdresser

folded sheets ,

and made sure that people behaved properly
in Mrs Crumple's launderette.

They also kept the baby fed . . .

and cheerful . . .

and clean.

At the end of the day they
were tired but happy.

Mrs Crumple went to the quiet, peaceful

pond with her fishing gear.

She had a nice long sit-down, and a cup of tea and some jam sandwiches.

Then, feeling much refreshed, she caught a big fish and chased lots of small boys.

At the end of the day she was tired but happ

She thanked the frogs for her day off.

She went into her little back room and made
the frogs some fishpaste sandwiches
and opened a packet of squashed-fly biscuits.

Next morning the frogs said goodbye to
Mrs Crumple and thanked her for their
wonderfully quiet holiday.

They went back along the street and down the hill to the pond, where life is always too

exciting.

And whenever the frogs want a holiday, they
go back to Mrs Crumple's launderette and
give her a day off. It is THE most perfect place
for a frogs' holiday.